INHERITING A MYSTERY

PIPPA FINN MYSTERIES
BOOK ONE

POPPY BLYTHE

PUREREAD.COM

Copyright © 2024 PureRead Ltd

www.pureread.com

All rights reserved. No part of this publication may be reproduced, distributed or transmitted in any form or by any means, without prior written permission.

Publisher's Note: This is a work of fiction. Names, characters, places, and incidents are a product of the author's imagination. Locales and public names are sometimes used for atmospheric purposes. Any resemblance to actual people, living or dead, or to businesses, companies, events, institutions, or locales is completely coincidental.

CONTENTS

Dear reader, get ready for another great Cozy…	1
Chapter 1	3
Chapter 2	8
Chapter 3	17
Chapter 4	28
Chapter 5	45
Chapter 6	59
Chapter 7	69
Chapter 8	76
Our Gift To You	87

DEAR READER, GET READY FOR ANOTHER GREAT COZY...

READY TO SOLVE THE MYSTERY?

Turn the page and let's begin

1

Pippa Finn sighed as she picked up another letter and tore it open, flinging the envelope down into a waste paper basket. She blinked away the fatigue and ran a hand through her light brown hair. A few strands somehow always managed to escape the confines of her ponytail, which endlessly annoyed her. She quickly scanned the figures.

"It looks like SEEC is dropping. I think we should dump it," she said.

Clive Meredith shook his head without looking at her. He pushed his glasses up the bridge of his nose with his index finger. He was a tall man, but he stooped and rolled his shoulders forward. Sitting at a desk all day didn't help.

"It's going to climb. I have a feeling."

Pippa rolled her eyes. "You and your feelings. This is about patterns and equations, not about feelings. Feelings have no place in this world," she snapped. In truth feelings had little place in any of Pippa's world. She was focused on her job, and her relationship with Clive was one that was mutually beneficial rather than filled with passion. Her life was based on a cost-benefit ratio, and love was not going to unbalance that.

This time though, Clive did look up at her. "I think I was the one that told you that. Anyway, my feelings are based on experience about these things. People are going to panic and dump their stock, but that means it's going to be more valuable when things even out. These things ebb and flow. You can't just make a knee jerk reaction when something unexpected happens. I'm sure it is just an aberration."

Pippa sighed. He always had a way of talking to her as though she was a child, especially when it came to finances. He could never quite believe that she knew as much as him. "If you say so," she relented. It was never worth it to get into an argument with him. "I was thinking about expanding our portfolio though. The world is going greener and I think we should focus on some new up and coming companies to invest in. I don't want to miss out on a big boom again. I have some prospects that I think are interesting," she said, picking up the packages she had made on the companies she had researched. "A few of them even have offices here in London so we could go and look at them. I think it might be fun to get invested on the ground floor and see something grow for a change."

Clive glanced at it, but then went back to staring at his laptop screen. His face was illuminated in the bluish glow, and it made him look even paler than he usually was.

"Investing in start ups is always risky. I'm not sure that we should be doing that right now. We've had a lot of success in going for stable investments with gradual growth. Let's not rock the boat," he said. Pippa left the documents on the table in front of him, even though she knew he wasn't going to look at them. He never did anything unless he thought it was a good idea. He could never trust anyone else's judgment.

Pippa looked through the other envelopes that she had picked up in the mail and one caught her eye because it was addressed to Penelope Finn, which was odd because on most forms of communication she used her nickname, Pippa, which she felt was more modern and stylish than Penelope. She furrowed her brow as she opened it and read it like all the other letters.

"Wow," Pippa said. Clive did not take his eyes of the display of the stock market index, which showed a list of abbreviated companies and the history of their stocks divided by three months, six months, a year, three years, and five years. "I have a house," she said.

"What?" Clive asked.

"Apparently my grandfather died and left me a house. I can't even remember the last time I spoke to him," she said, and was then flushed with a spike of guilt at all the years that had passed in a blur. She remembered visiting her grandfather as a child, walking along the pier with the smell of salt and vinegar dousing her fingers after having fries, the gulls cawing, the air fresh and cool as it washed over the beach. It was a memory that almost seemed as if it was from another life. Pippa had not been that innocent child for a long time, and she knew she didn't deserve this inheritance.

"That's good. We could sell it, make a nice profit," Clive said.

"Yeah… I… I guess I should go and see what kind of state it's in. I think I'm going to have to take a trip for a few days."

"Okay, well, let me know when you've made the arrangements. I'll hold the fort here," he said. Pippa failed to notice that he didn't even offer his condolences. She rose from the table, still clutching the letter, and staggered to the bathroom. She twisted the faucet and watched the water spray out. She cupped her hands underneath it and then splashed her face, looking in the mirror at her reflection. She had deep brown eyes, a button nose, and a slender face. When she looked into her own eyes she saw guilt, guilt at being a stranger to her grandfather, and guilt at not knowing that he had even died.

It was a link to the past that she had not thought about for a long time, but one that existed nonetheless. She had always assumed there would be another day when she would see him again, but now there were no more days. She became stunned, and there was an ache in her chest as she went into the bedroom and pulled the sheets over her. She didn't even get undressed. She lay there with her eyes open, thinking about the past. For a long time she just lay there, thinking about how sad it was that her grandfather had died alone.

But even so he had still left his cottage to her. He had still been thinking about her, even after all this time. There was something about that which broke her heart, her heart that had been hardened over years of focus and determination, years of clawing her way up a corporate job and trying to grasp the modern world in her hands. But this shocking development was going to take her away from all that, away from London with its stylish bars, high rise skyscrapers, and cosmopolitan lifestyle, away to the coastal town of Burlybottom on Sea.

2

The drive to the southern coast took Pippa a number of hours. Her sleek car slipped along the motorway and through the forest lanes. She scowled when she was delayed behind a slow moving tractor that crawled along the road, and tapped her fingers in annoyance whenever the SATNAV took her in the wrong direction because the web of roads that made up this part of the world was a tangled mess. It used to be that her mother would always bring her here in the summer for a vacation. When Pippa crested a hill she saw the sea rippling on the horizon. It was a shade darker than the sky, and the waves danced, dappled by the sunlight. The roads were old and narrow, and there was an annoying one way system in the town that she thought was there to dissuade people from driving more than anything else. Thankfully it was short enough to walk across. Pippa sighed as she passed the roundabout and looked out along the pier, which had seemed to stretch halfway into the ocean when she was younger. Gulls cawed and circled overheard, while cafes and stores peppered the road opposite the beach. The sand was golden and the tide left behind a shadow as it ebbed and flowed. In the distance she could see the rising mountains curving around the land, the stone white, the ridged surface looking like the brow of a stern teacher.

She passed through the town and drove toward this coastal region, where her grandfather's cottage was located. When she pulled up it was just as she remembered, although the paintwork had faded. The doorframe and windowsills were blue, while the front garden was filled with all kinds of potted plants. As a girl she had gone around with a watering can and sprinkled them with water. Her grandfather used to tell her that she was making it rain. A smile twitched, but did not fully form. Once again she was filled with the feeling that the memory had been from someone else's life. At some point that girl had grown up to become Pippa, and she wasn't sure when exactly it had occurred.

She got out of the car and opened the gate, which hung on its hinges. She didn't bother closing it behind her. Just before she reached the door, the next door neighbor's door opened up and two women popped their heads out. Pippa didn't recognize them. They both wore glasses, one had a pair of circle glasses with thick rims, while the other had narrow glasses. They wore flowery dresses and their hair was streaked with grey, while their skin was lined with wrinkles.

"Are you here to sell the house?" the lady on the right asked.

"Or are you here to inspect it? We did try and tell him to keep it clean, but he never listened to us. He wouldn't get rid of anything of his at all."

"I'm sorry, who are you?" Pippa asked in a brusque tone.

"I'm Martha," one said.

"And I'm Mindy," the other one replied. They spoke almost in unison and the longer Pippa stared the more she could see the resemblance. "We've been curious about what's going to happen to the house. We don't like to think about who might move in. You can never tell nowadays. I mean, I don't bear any ill will toward people at all, but we do have a certain way of life and I wouldn't like to think that anyone loud is going to move in beside us. We do like our naps, don't we Martha?"

"Oh we do," Martha said, nodding enthusiastically.

"Well I don't know who might be living here, and in fact I don't know what is happening with the house. I'm Pippa, Gordon's granddaughter," Pippa said.

"Oh you're Penny? Oh Gordon did mention you a lot! It's a pleasure to meet you. If you need anything don't hesitate to let us know. I always did hope that some of his family would come around. There are so many questions I have about him," Mindy said.

"What kind of questions?" Pippa said through gritted teeth. She had the key placed in the lock already, ready to enter the cottage.

"Oh, you know, the usual things. He always was so reclusive about his past. I always got the sense of mystery around him. You know you get that sense around certain men?" Mindy said.

"Oh I do Mindy, I do, we used to have him over for cups of tea, but there were things he would not talk about."

"I'm sure he had his reasons. We have been a private family. I suppose it must be a trait I got from him. Anyway, I doubt I shall be troubling you for too long. I'm only here to inspect the house and then I'll be out of your hair. As for who might live here in the end, I have no control over that. I haven't decided if I'm going to sell the cottage or not yet," Pippa said. She then twisted the key in the lock and opened it, walking in just as Mindy went to speak again. She managed to get half a sentence out of her mouth before Pippa disappeared.

Pippa breathed a sigh of relief as she closed the door behind her. The last thing she wanted was to be accosted by a pair of nosy neighbors, and by the looks of them they were twins. There was always something odd about twins, Pippa thought. It had irked her that they referred to her as Penny as well. That was the name that her grandfather had always called her by. It felt wrong to hear it on the lips of these two strangers. It didn't help her guilt either, to know that Gordon had been talking about her, probably talking about how proud he was of her and how she had a big successful career in London, while also reminiscing about old times. Pippa closed eyes and shook the thoughts away. There was no sense in getting upset about things that couldn't be helped. It wasn't as though she could apologize to him. Better just to get on with what she was here to do and then get back to London where she could carry on with her life.

The door to the cottage led into a narrow hallway. There were framed pictures on the wall, and a coat stand. Her grandfather's jackets were still hanging there, which seemed eerie to her. Two rooms split off from the hallway, a lounge and a spare room, while it ended with the kitchen and a staircase that led upstairs. As soon as she inspected the rooms she groaned. They were filled with clutter; small ornaments that looked like they belonged in an antique store, shelves filled with tattered books and old newspapers and magazines, letters that formed a pile, and all kinds of things that spoke of the man who had lived here. It was such a contrast to her own orderly home, where if something did not serve a purpose then it had no place in her home. Any book she read was swiftly passed on, the photos she possessed were all stored on her phone and laptop, and she only had enough clothes to get her through the work week, with a few outfits for special occasions. Her grandfather had evidently been a hoarder.

It didn't get any better as she explored the house. The kitchen was filled with all kinds of culinary equipment that might never have been used, as well as far too many plates and glasses and sets of cutlery for a man who lived alone. Upstairs the bedroom was again filled with clutter.

"Did you ever hear of the concept of throwing things away Grandad?" she muttered under her breath. Her attention was caught by a book on the bedside table though. The page was turned three quarters of the way through. It struck her that Gordon hadn't finished it before he died, and something about that seemed unutterably sad. She picked the book up and flicked through the pages. It was some thriller about the army, probably Gordon wanted to relive his glory days. She put the book back and tested the mattress. It creaked, the old springs moaning like a pensioner with arthritis, and she sighed, wishing that she had been able to bring her memory foam mattress with her. She would have to try and do some yoga to ensure that her back did not get too badly damaged. At least she wasn't going to be here for long.

It was going to be arduous to go through all the knick knacks Gordon had collected. He had probably held onto all these things in the hope that one of them might be valuable, as so many other people had. It showed a lack of understanding of how the economic market worked. People who put their hope into ornaments were fools. By sheer chance one of them might have been worth something, given how many Gordon possessed, but it was unlikely. She might just have to throw them out in order to make sure the sale went quickly.

It was a little late by the time she arrived in Burlybottom on Sea, and by the time she had explored the house and the garden, as well as the shed within the garden, she was quite tired. When she was out in the garden she saw the twins peering out of their kitchen window, although they quickly scurried away when Pippa glared at them.

She crawled into bed and adjusted her position a number of times to try and get comfortable, but nothing worked. In the end she had to endure the lumpy mattress and hope that her tiredness was such that she would drift away into sleep.

It was more difficult than she assumed it would be though. She was used to living in London, which was alive with noise, even in the depths of night. There was always the rush of a car or the rumble of the tube, or even the roar of a plane flying overhead. In her clustered apartment building she could hear the ambient noise of other people's lives bleeding through the walls and ceiling too, and over time these had come to be reassuring. But out in the cottage the village was quiet. There was nothing to hear but the echoes in her own mind, and she did not like the thoughts that were rattling around. She heard other noises too, sighs and moans from the old house, eerie noises that gave rise to old stories of ghouls and ghosts haunting the modern world. It had been a long time since she had felt this alone, and she did not like it at all.

To try and alleviate her loneliness she pulled out her cell phone and called Clive, but he did not answer. There was nobody else she could call, and her phone signal wasn't quite catching the Internet, so she couldn't even while her time away by catching up on any gossip or drama on social media. She sighed as she flung her phone down and gazed up at the ceiling, wondering if this was poetic justice to how Gordon had felt, abandoned by his own family, left to rot in this cluttered cottage.

The noises began again, this time more insistent. It was as though some creature was scratching at the walls of the cottage. Pippa suddenly wondered what had happened to her grandfather. She had seen enough horror movies to have her imagination inspired by gruesome images, but she told herself that she was being ridiculous. She also remembered a piece of advice that she had heard; that if she ever had problems falling asleep it was better to get up and do something rather than lay in bed, because it was a way to trick the body and reset it when you returned to bed. It also gave her an excuse to go and investigate the noises and reassure herself that there wasn't anything amiss downstairs. She clutched her phone in her hand and activated the flashlight mode, shining it ahead of her, creating a glaring halo that spread out before her.

She crept downstairs, taking each step one at a time. Her footsteps were light, but even so they still creaked. She almost stumbled on one as the stairs were uneven and she hadn't quite remembered their quirks, even though as a girl she would have been fleet footing down them. When she was on level ground she exhaled and was about to turn, but she was too late. There was a flurry of movement and something leapt from the darkness at her, striking from out of nowhere.

3

Pippa yelped and raised her hands to try and protect herself. In the moment of panic the lessons she had learned in self defense classes drifted from her mind. She was certain it was some violent attacker that had been hiding in the house, perhaps some squatter that had been using Gordon's cottage for shelter. She cried out and then went to stagger back, before she realized that the person who had grappled her was now pawing at her, and as she reached out she felt the fur and then heard the panting breaths, and then felt the tongue licking her palms. She shone the light down and felt entirely foolish for being afraid of a dog. Its eyes were wide, dark orbs, while its ears were drooping and its fur was a beautiful cascade of chocolate brown curls. It settled on its haunches and looked up at her expectantly. Pippa merely stared at it. Her landlord did not allow pets, and she had never had the time for animals anyway.

"I don't know how you got in here, and I'm not sure what you're doing here. Go," she said, pointing back toward the garden, from where she assumed the dog came in. She would have to check the doors to make sure that everything was secure. She couldn't just have random dogs coming in. The dog did not move though. Pippa placed her hands on her hips and furrowed her brow. She was about to command the dog to leave again when suddenly there was a rapping knock on the door, which startled her and almost made her jump out of her skin. She turned around and saw the silhouette of a man standing in the doorway. Pippa's first instinct was to flee back upstairs and pretend that none of this had happened, but whoever was there had likely seen the glare of her flashlight, and if the dog could get in then so, could the man. She wasn't about to be naïve though; she went into the spare room and picked up a hefty ornament. The dog followed behind her, its paws thudding against the floorboards.

She opened the door a crack and peered up at a ruggedly handsome man with a disarming smile.

"Good evening ma'am, I'm John Clarkson, I'm sorry to disturb you," he said in a low, rumbling tone that made her weak at the knees. Pippa clenched her jaw in an effort to try and regain control of her feelings. She never usually suffered this effect. John had a square jaw and blue eyes, with a thick head of hair that was like a mane. He wasn't like the kind of men she knew in London, the men with big brains and thin arms, wearing glasses and shirts instead of being a man of nature. John had broad shoulders and thick biceps, and from the way he carried himself he wasn't lacking in confidence either. When she glanced down she noticed that he was holding a leash.

"What do you want?" she asked, still gripping the ornament tightly.

"Well, I've been looking after Jasper here since Gordon died. He ran away from my farm though. I know I should have kept him tied up, but he really doesn't like it and I don't have the heart to be cruel to him, especially not after what he's been through. I figured he'd come back here, although I didn't expect to find anyone in his house."

"I'm Gordon's granddaughter, Pippa."

"It's a pleasure to meet you ma'am," he said, nodding to her. By appearance he looked to be just a few years older than her, but by his manners he seemed from another generation entirely. Then again she was used to men who were in touch with their youth. "I really am sorry to disturb you. I just wanted to make sure that Jasper was alright."

"I'm sure he'll be quite well now that you're here to take him back. I really can't look after him. I'm not going to be here for long," Pippa said. At this point the dog – Jasper – nuzzled into her legs and forced her to open the door. She quickly thrust the ornament behind her, as though embarrassed that she had been ready to attack John. Jasper licked Pippa's hand even though she tried to take it away. It was an odd tickling sensation and Pippa found herself having to stifle a laugh.

"I don't know, it looks like he's quite at home here," John said, and then chuckled to himself as he walked away, after placing the leash in Pippa's hand. Pippa couldn't quite believe that he was actually leaving this dog with her and she took a couple of steps down the garden path.

"You can't leave! Take this dog with you!" she cried.

"Jasper will be fine. I'm sure you'll take care of him. You are family, after all. It was nice to make your acquaintance, I'm sure I'll be seeing you around," he said, and then sauntered away. Pippa looked aghast. She was staring into space as Jasper circled her feet, and then he went back into the cottage, waiting at the doorway for her expectantly. Pippa groaned. This trip was turning into a nightmare and she trudged back inside, flinging the leash onto the couch before storming upstairs. Jasper followed and settled at the end of the bed, as though that was his place.

Whether she liked it or not, Pippa eventually did fall asleep far more easily with Jasper at the end of the bed, and she found herself thinking about John more than she would have liked.

When Pippa awoke in the morning she heard Jasper making fretting noises. He was going at something in the kitchen and she dreaded the thought that he might have found a rat or something. She went downstairs and found him pawing at an empty water bowl. She filled it with water and he lapped it up eagerly. Then she searched the cupboards for some dog food and found that as well, and Jasper greedily tucked into it. Pippa pinched the bridge of her nose and tried to think about the agenda for the day. She needed to make an inventory of everything that Gordon had so she could properly appraise the value of it, but that was going to take time.

Pippa had never been one to delay the inevitable, but when she went to get started Jasper headed straight for the door and began to scratch at it.

"I can't take you for a walk right now Jasper. I'm busy," she said. Jasper didn't care. He kept scratching and then he came into the room with her and circled her legs, making it impossible for her to do anything. She threw her hands up. "Fine, let's go for a walk and then maybe you'll calm down. Maybe we'll run into that farmer and I can give him a piece of my mind. Who does he think he is, leaving you with me?" she shook her head and picked up the leash, bending down to put it around Jasper's neck. Jasper ducked and weaved, making it difficult for Pippa to put it on.

"I don't know how Grandad ever put up with you," she muttered, eventually managing to get the leash around Jasper's neck. The dog whimpered and looked forlorn as he sat there. It was almost enough for Pippa to feel sorry for him. She took hold of the leash and then walked out of the cottage, although as she turned out of the gate Jasper sprang forward and it quickly became clear that he was walking her rather than her walking him. No matter how much she struggled to try and get control of the leash, Jasper was more insistent. He led her down the winding road to the seafront and she ran past a few villagers, blushing emphatically as Jasper whisked her by them.

They ended up in a pub called *The Highwayman*. The door was open and Jasper zipped in. He went right up to the bar, which was a long curved counter stretching through the long room. A variety of bottles were displayed behind the bar, while tables peppered the room. At the far wall was a wide hearth and various paintings hung on the walls, although Pippa only spared a glance at them. She didn't mind that Jasper had taken her to this pub though because she could have used a drink and something to eat.

"Jasper! I didn't think I'd see you today, and who is this that you've brought with you?"

"I'm Pippa," she said.

"And I'm Braw Ben McGraw, welcome to Burlybottom by Sea," he said. Pippa cringed when she heard the name. She wondered how anyone could say it with a straight face. He reached down and pulled out a packet of pork scratching. He plucked out a handful and tossed one in the direction of Jasper, who plucked it out of the air. Then he shoved one in his mouth. His chewing made a horrible crunching noise and Pippa shuddered. It sounded like his teeth were cracking. Braw Ben was a ruddy man with a stocky build. His hair was retreating from his scalp, but he made up for it with a bushy orange beard. His gaze passed between Jasper and her, and then he furrowed his brow a little.

"Are you Gordon's daughter?" he asked.

Pippa didn't know whether he was insulting her by thinking that she was older, or complimenting her grandfather by suggesting he was younger. "I'm his granddaughter," she said in a strident tone, arching her head up.

"Ah, that explains the family resemblance, and why you have Jasper here by your side," he said, and then tossed Jasper another pork scratching. Pippa wasn't sure this was healthy for an animal, or a human for that matter, but she decided not to say anything.

"Yes, well, I don't think that family resemblances count for much," Pippa said.

"There's no finer honor," Braw Ben muttered under his breath. Pippa chose to ignore him. She didn't see a menu anywhere, but she placed an order anyway.

"I was hoping I could have some breakfast here. I would like some gluten free bread, an avocado yoghurt, and a fruit smoothie please, preferably something with mango in it," she said, wondering if this place would actually take a credit card or if it was still archaic enough to use cash. She wasn't sure if she had many coins jingling about in her purse. Braw Ben looked at her for a moment and she wondered if he had actually understood her. She was about to place her order again when he burst out laughing and tossed his head back. It was the kind of laugh that took hold of his entire body. She had only known him for a matter of minutes, but Braw Ben didn't seem like a man who did anything by half. His laugh was a living, writhing thing that danced through the air to its own melody and he actually had to wipe away a tear. Pippa stood there, looking indignant.

"Oh you can really tell when city folk come to town," Braw Ben said, and just about managed to calm down. Pippa waited for the laughter to abate. She shouldn't have expected that a place like this would be civilized enough to have progressive foods, especially considering Braw Ben was still chucking pork scratching down his throat. Pippa shuddered to think what other unhealthy, greasy foods were the snacks of choice for people in this town. It was a wonder with a diet like this that her grandfather had lasted as long as he did.

"I'm not going to stay for very long," Pippa hissed, letting Braw Ben know that she did not have much respect for him in turn. Braw Ben's laugh settled into his usual wheezing breath and then he leaned on the counter, getting closer to her. He thrust out a thick finger and she could see the crumbs of pork scratching in his beard.

"I suppose you don't want any of the treasure then," he said in a mysterious tone.

Now it was Pippa's turn to laugh. "And what treasure would that be?" she asked, not expecting an answer, but Braw Ben was ready to give her one.

"It's a tale that has been going around the village for some time now. I'm surprised your grandfather never told it to you. Apparently there's some buried jewels along the coast. Some people say a meteor fell from the skies carrying massive shards of jewels, while other people claim that people brought it from a faraway land and then mysteriously disappeared before they could make use of it. Either way, area people are sure there's something out there, buried in the rock, and that's not to mention all the strange happenings that have gone on in the hills and the forests around this place."

"What strange goings on?" Pippa asked, frowning.

Braw Ben shrugged. "Strange noises and figures at night, tracks found on the ground that have no explanation. If you want to know more you should ask Mindy and Martha Marlow. They'll know everything."

"Yes, I suppose they would," Pippa said, remembering how the twins seemed intent on discovering what she was up to. Pippa imagined they showed the same fascination with anyone in their immediate vicinity. People like them often had nothing going on in their own lives so had to create fantastical stories about other people to keep themselves entertained. Life could be slow in a place like this, but really, strange tales like this was simply too much. Pippa shook her head and brushed away the fable.

"I'm quite sure that anything has a rational explanation. These tales just get passed along in folklore and end up being crazier the more people say them. It's just a huge game of Chinese Whispers, and I don't want any part of it. I'm just here to sort out my grandfather's things and then I shall return to the city," she said.

Braw Ben shrugged again and sighed. He leaned back, returning himself from his full height. "It's a shame, there's treasure out there and someone has to find it. I always thought Gordon knew something about it. He had this look in his eyes whenever the subject came up. A tightlipped one, your grandfather was. Never liked playing cards with him."

The comment brought back a memory to Pippa's mind. It seemed as though the longer she remained here the more her childhood was coming back to her. She wasn't sure if this was a good thing or a bad thing. She remembered sitting at a table with her grandfather while he explained the rules of various card games to her. Looking back now she could see that he let her win, but he was always patient with her and it had been too long since she had held a deck of cards in her hand. The only cards she handled now were business cards.

"He was a good man though, used to come in here a lot. I guess he needed the company," Braw Ben continued. Pippa wondered if there was a veiled insult there. "He will be missed. I'm sorry I can't cater to your needs, but if you want to come in later for a drink I'll be glad to share a toast to him," Braw Ben said.

"Perhaps I shall," Pippa said, although she had no intention of stepping into that pub again. The smell of pork and ale clung to her clothes and she was glad to leave so that she might get some fresh air. Braw Ben also bid farewell to Jasper as he followed Pippa outside. This time Pippa took a firm hold of the leash and bent down, wagging her finger in front of Jasper's face.

"You are not going to make a fool of me again Jasper. I am the human and I am in control here. We will walk where I say we're going to walk, okay?" she said, while looking into the dog's gorgeous brown eyes. A couple of people passed by and cast a strange look her away. Pippa scowled again. The last thing she needed was to get a reputation as someone who was talking to animals as if they could understand her. She muttered a curse under her breath and then walked away.

4

The thought of food had made her stomach rumble, so she scanned the immediate surroundings for a sign of a café that might actually sell something edible. She saw a white building called *The Tea Pot Pit* and headed toward it, hoping that she might be able to get a sandwich, even if the bread wasn't gluten free. It was a short, brisk walk, and this time Jasper was behaving himself. Perhaps the pork scratching had calmed him down. Pippa had a brief thought about the story Braw Ben had told her, but then dismissed it and wondered why she was wasting her time thinking about it. After all, he was probably just making fun of her, trying to play a trick on the naïve girl from the city. However, just for a moment she did cast her mind back and think about whether Gordon had indeed told her a story like that, but if he had it did not come to mind.

She entered the café and was pleased; this was far more her style. There was a small counter with potted plants behind it, and round tables with prim chairs tucked underneath them. The owner was a young woman, probably about Pippa's age. She had tawny brown hair that reached her chin and a wide smile that defined her face.

"Good morning, what can I do for you today, oh hello Jasper," she said, bounding out from behind the counter and greeting the dog with a lot of affection. Jasper clearly knew her as well, as he licked her face. Pippa stood there awkwardly, not entirely sure how to cope with someone showing this much open affection to a dog. "I've got something for you, hold on for a moment," she said, and then quickly glanced at Pippa. "I'll be with you in a second, take a seat anywhere you like."

Pippa pulled out a chair near the window and sat down. Jasper craned his neck in the direction the kitchen. The owner emerged and handed a small cut of meat to Jasper, who swallowed it whole. Did everyone in this place treat Jasper with food? No wonder he was itching to get out on a walk. He would probably put on half a stone by the time he was done with all the cafes and restaurants along the way.

"Do you know John?" the owner asked.

Pippa thought for a moment, and then remembered that it was the farmer's name. This girl must have thought that she knew John, since she had Jasper. "No, well, we met briefly last night. I'm Pippa, I'm Gordon's granddaughter. I'm here to look over his house. I suppose that includes Jasper, or at least he seems to think so," Pippa said, looking down at the dog with a wary smile.

"I'm Callie, it's a pleasure to meet you. Any relative of Gordon is a friend of mine," she said with a happy smile, but then it flickered and faded away. "I am sorry about what happened. What can I get you? It's on the house."

"Oh, no, please, there's no need for that."

"No, I insist. Gordon was a regular here and it's the least I can do," Callie said. "Take a look at the menu."

Pippa took out the printed cream card and glanced at the traditional menu, eventually plumping for a tuna and cucumber sandwich with a lemonade. Callie nodded and went to make it straight away. It was a quiet café and evidently the morning crowd had not arrived yet as everything was quiet. When Callie returned she pulled out a seat and joined Pippa.

"Have you come from far away?" Callie asked.

"London," Pippa said after taking a bite of her sandwich. Even though the bread was not gluten free she was still glad to get some food into her stomach, and even after just one bite she felt her mood improving. There was another pang of guilt though. She wished she could have said Shanghai or New York, somewhere truly far away that would have been a better excuse for her to not visit or attend the funeral. If Callie was thinking the same thing then she didn't say it.

"Oh that's wonderful! I would love to live in London. It must be so filled with adventure!" Callie said, her eyes sparkling. Pippa was about to disabuse her of that notion before she caught herself. There was no sense in shattering this woman's illusion of what London was like. Instead, Pippa feigned a smile.

"It can be," she said.

"I'd love to go to all sorts of places. I sit here all day and look out to the sea and dream about what's out there. I doubt I'll see it though. I couldn't leave this place," she spoke with a melancholy sigh. Pippa could identify with her. She knew what it was like to feel trapped. When that happened you could do nothing but try and smash your way out. "It's why I loved Gordon coming in. He always had some exotic story about the different places he had been."

"Really?" Pippa asked with surprise. As far as she remembered he hadn't traveled much.

"Yes, during his time in the war," Callie explained. Pippa nodded. Ah yes, the war. He hadn't spoken much about it when she was younger. She supposed that they had lost touch before she had become old enough to know about those stories. Now she was going to have to hear them second hand from someone who might well have been his surrogate granddaughter. At least he hadn't been too alone though. With Braw Ben and Callie, Gordon had people to keep him company.

She told herself this in the hope that it would alleviate the guilt she felt at not spending more time with him.

It did not.

"I'm glad he had someone to talk to. I did keep meaning to see him, but work was just so busy," Pippa lied.

"I can imagine what it must be like in London. I bet it's like living in another world compared to this place," Callie said with a slight chuckle. "It's funny; I used to tell myself that I was never going to end up staying here, but then one thing leads to another and, well, you never can predict what's going to happen in life, can you? Are you staying in town for long?"

"I'm not sure yet. I'm not intending to. I'm really just here to look over the cottage and see what the state of it is."

"Oh," Callie's face fell, "Well, while you're in town feel free to pop in any time you like. You're always welcome, as is Jasper, of course."

"Thank you," Pippa smiled, realizing that she wasn't quite deserving of this reception. "Could I ask you something, something about my grandfather?"

"Of course," Callie said.

"What was he like? I mean, with people. Was he happy? Was he well liked?"

"Oh yes. I can't imagine that anyone wouldn't have liked Gordon. He was always out here, walking Jasper up and down, and whenever you needed anything done he was always happy to do it. He fixed the door for me because it was sticking, and he was always helping out Braw Ben with some bits and pieces. The Misses Marlow wouldn't leave him alone either. He was a real part of this community. He will be missed," the smile fell from her face and was replaced by a maudlin expression, and her sigh was heavy. Pippa felt sympathy for her, and then checked herself. She was the family member, she was the granddaughter. She was the one who should have been feeling what Callie was feeling, and yet she wasn't, because Gordon hadn't been a part of her life, not for a long time. This hole that Callie and the other people felt in Burlybottom on Sea was something that Pippa wouldn't know, and that made her sad.

Callie had been lost in thought for a moment too, but she shook that away and forced the smile to appear back on her face. "Well, I'm sure that Gordon wouldn't want us moping around. He'd tell us that we only go around once so we have to make the most of it."

"Yes," Pippa said, pretending that she knew one of Gordon's frequent sayings.

"Could I ask you about someone else as well?" Pippa asked, trying to change the subject while she had the chance. "It's about John Clarkson, the farmer."

"Oh yes," Callie said, and clearly warmed at the mention of the name. Pippa wondered if there was anything romantic between the two of them. She didn't see a ring on Callie's finger, although she couldn't remember if she had seen one on John's or not.

"Well, I just wondered what kind of person he was really. He came searching for Jasper last night, and then he left Jasper with me! I don't know what he was thinking, but I am really unprepared to look after a dog."

"Oh, well, I'm sure he didn't mean anything by it. He probably just liked the idea of Jasper being back at home for a few nights. I'm sure that he'll be happy to take Jasper back again when you leave, if not then bring Jasper around here."

"Thank you, I do appreciate it," Pippa said, and she meant it.

"No problem," Callie said. Another customer entered so Callie went to greet them. Pippa watched her and wondered if this bubbly personality was something that came naturally to her or if it was something that she forced for the sake of her job. Pippa polished off her sandwich and then gave the leash a tug, showing Jasper that it was time to move again.

Pippa had walked a few yards down the road when she noticed a vicar approaching her. There was no mistaking his distinguishable clothes. He was a middle aged man with greying hair and kind eyes. Pippa felt a knot tighten in her stomach as he came closer, for she hadn't had much use for church over the past few years. She knew that Clive would have a good laugh when he found out that she had a conversation with a vicar. The vicar smiled and petted Jasper, and then greeted her.

"You must be Penny," he said. "I'm George Dimbleby, I believe I recognize you from when you used to visit as a child. Oh, I was so young then, having just arrived here," he said with a glow.

"I go by Pippa now," she said, smiling politely. She didn't much remember him at all.

"Oh, very well, it's a pleasure to see you again."

"How did you know I was here?" Pippa asked.

"Word gets around, especially with Martha and Mindy around," the vicar said. Pippa rolled her eyes. She should have suspected that those busybodies would have been on the telephone to all their friends and probably everyone else in the village. Pippa hadn't wanted to garner any attention during her brief stay here, yet it seemed that everyone wanted to stop her and say something about her grandfather. Were they all just trying to send her on a guilt trip?

"I suppose it does."

"They don't mean any harm, they just like to share the news," George said, clasping his hands together. He had a soothing voice that Pippa presumed had served him well during his career, although she was careful not allowing it to goad her into revealing anything she didn't want to. "Anyway, I just wanted to come and check on how you're doing. I know that losing a loved one can be difficult."

"I'm doing just fine, thank you. I'm only here to sort out his belongings and things."

"Of course, of course. I just want you to know that I'm always available if you need a chat. Gordon was such a stalwart in our church. I'm sure I've never met a man like him, and it's going to be a while before we can replace him as a tenor in the choir." He leaned in closer and lowered his voice to a clandestine whisper. "I also wanted you to know that if you want to come and pay your respects that is fine as well. I understand you were not able to make it to the funeral, so if at any point you want to come and say goodbye to your grandfather then let me know and I will arrange it," he said.

"Thank you," Pippa said, although she was troubled by the offer. It hadn't actually occurred to her that he might be buried here and that she should go and see him. It was clear that all these people she encountered cared for

Gordon more than she had. She excused herself from the vicar's company and returned to the cottage, sinking into a chair and holding her head in her hands.

She had pitied her grandfather when she had seen his house, but from what she had learned today it was clear that he had a full life. He was trusted around town and popular. He was a part of the choir and was still helping people with odd jobs even into his old age. His was not a life to be pitied, but one to be envied, and although Pippa was much younger than Gordon it got her thinking about her own mortality as well. If she died would people speak so kindly about her? She wasn't sure. She was just another face in a sea of them in London. The interactions she had in bars and restaurants were fleeting and hollow. Her friends would miss her, but those were few and far between. Many of them had been lost in the ether when she had gotten busy with her career. The people she did business with might be shocked to hear of her passing, but they would soon find someone else to liaise with. Her footprint on the world would be small, and she suddenly felt extremely lonely and lost.

She busied herself by looking through some of her grandfather's things. There was lots of war memorabilia as well as photos from his time in the army. He looked far different than she remembered. This was the version of him that she had never known, a man who had lived a life long before she was born. He looked fresh faced, probably too young to fight in a war in truth, but then wasn't that true of every man? He had defended his country, sacrificed so much, and what did he get for his troubles? A granddaughter who couldn't even be bothered to call him on the phone. She pinched the bridge of her nose to try and force away the band of tension that wrapped around her forehead, but it didn't work. She needed to speak to someone.

She pulled out her phone and held it to her ear, still preferring to talk this way rather than have the call on speakerphone. This time Clive did answer, and she was thankful for it.

"How's it going down there by the sea?" he asked.

"Oh it's fine. There are some... interesting characters."

"I bet. It must be like being in a zoo or something. Do they even have the Internet down there yet?"

"It's not that far from London Clive," she said. Clive chuckled to himself. He always found bitter things amusing. It was something that she had never quite been able to understand.

"Have you found anything worthwhile in the house, or is it all junk?"

"I think most of it is junk, but some of it might be interesting. There's a lot about his career in the war."

"Ah yes, a remembrance of a time when people were forced to lay down their lives. I'm so glad we live in a more enlightened age. Listen, are you going to be back by the weekend? I was thinking of having a dinner party with Edgar and Joyce."

"I probably will be, I'm just trying to figure things out here. He had a lot of stuff. Once I do that then I can actually look at the state of the cottage properly and estimate how much I could get for it."

"Good, good, I suppose the English coast isn't what it used to be. It's not as though we could use it as a holiday home. I do hope you come back, soon though. I don't like the thought of you being away from London for too long. I get worried that you're going to forget how the modern world works," he laughed again. Pippa pursed her lips and waited for him to stop so that she could be heard over the laughter.

"I'm not going to be too long. Just hold the plans for the dinner party for now. Listen, there was something I wanted to talk to you about though… do you think I was a bad granddaughter for ignoring him?"

"You didn't ignore him, you just didn't go to see him. It's not like he reached out to you that often. It's not your fault that he didn't have email or text, I mean, how can anyone expect people to keep in contact by a phone nowadays?" he asked.

"I know, but it's just that being around here… it sounds like he had a full life and people really liked being around him. I just feel like I might have missed out and that I should have made more of an effort. I mean, they had a memorial service for him and I wasn't even there. None of his family was here."

"That's not your fault Pippa. You can't feel guilty for having your own life. You've put a lot of time and effort into making yourself a success. I'm sure he would have understood that. He fought in the war for goodness' sake, he knows about sacrifice. He fought for your right to make a success out of yourself in a free world so I don't think he would have been too upset. He would have been proud if anything. It's just the way it goes anyway. Being tethered to a family is a thing of the past. We're not living in Victorian times where we're all cramped in one terraced house. We spread across the world. We're more independent. It's just the way of life. I'm the same with my parents, so don't let these people get to you. I'm sure it's just that wherever you are seems like it's from another time. He clearly wasn't moping around because he had his own life, as you said. Don't be too hard on yourself."

"Okay," Pippa said, seeing the wisdom in his words, although it didn't quite sit right with her. Clive then said that he had to leave, which plunged her into silence again. The call ended and she looked down at Jasper, and then her stomach began to rumble.

∼

Pippa took Jasper for another walk along the seafront as she went to fetch some fish and chips. She was hit with a wave of nostalgia as she was handed the meal. Jasper walked alongside her as she went to the beachfront and sat on a bench, looking out to the horizon. The water met the sea far, far away. It was a sight that was impossible to find in London, and was a reminder that the capital city was not the center of the world. She ate her meal and then returned to the cottage, thinking about the girl she used to be when she came here and the woman she had dreamed of growing into. Had she achieved all she wanted to achieve? Had she become that person who had existed only in her mind?

Upon returning to the cottage she languished in silence before she went to bed. Because of the sheer amount of Gordon's things she was going to have to spend more time here than she initially thought. Jasper accompanied her up to her room again and this night she hoped she would get better sleep.

∼

She twisted and turned in bed, and was drifting in and out of sleep when she heard a sharp noise. She jolted awake and her eyes shot open. She strained her ears and tried to tell herself that it was just the sounds of the house. Old cottages like this would creak and moan and seem alive, but it was only the old foundations straining against age. Pippa's breath was shallow though, and her chest was tight. Once fear took hold in a mind it was so difficult to dispel it. Every sound, real or imagined, suddenly became some creature skittering in the depths of the cottage. She was frozen in bed again, before she told herself that, just like last night, it was probably nothing. It might even have been the farmer coming around again to check on Jasper. She flung off the sheets of the bed and was about to charge downstairs, when suddenly Jasper growled.

Okay, so if she was suspicious it was one thing, but Jasper? Animals had a certain sense about this kind of thing, didn't they? She bent low and tried to listen if he would growl again, and she found herself wishing that he could speak. His wide eyes betrayed nothing. She pressed her lips together and thought about what to do. There was no sense in calling the police because she didn't know if there was anything to be worried about yet. She could try and stay in her room, but she hated being a victim of fear and she would never be able to sleep. Besides, if someone was creeping around downstairs then they might well creep upstairs as well. At least if she went down to confront them she might be able to take them by surprise. They were in the wrong after all, intruding in a place that didn't belong to them.

Giving what she had learned about her grandfather though she wouldn't have been surprised to learn that he had allowed someone to stay here free of charge, not that she had seen any sign that he had a guest.

"Come on Jasper," she whispered, deciding to venture downstairs. She crept down the steps, this time searching her memory to remember which ones creaked and which ones didn't. Jasper's steps were light enough to not provoke any noise. She was about to pull her phone out and shine the flashlight again, when suddenly she heard a noise. It came from the spare room. She stood in the doorway and saw a silhouetted figure in the middle of the room. For a moment she was stunned and just stood there, staring at the individual.

Then Jasper barked.

The figure, who looked to have the frame of a man, although she couldn't be sure, dropped whatever he was holding and swung around. He wore a black balaclava, and as soon as he saw Pippa and Jasper standing in the doorway he bolted toward the window, crashing through ornaments that she had carefully organized. Some of them shattered as he threw himself out of the window. Pippa ran toward the door and flung it open. She could see him running and she ran down the garden path, her heart hammering in her chest. Jasper raced to the edge of the path, sniffing the air.

Pippa joined him and looked to the horizon. She strained her eyes, but the intruder had disappeared into the shadows. If she was braver she might well have followed the scent that Jasper had caught, but she was too afraid. The man could have attacked her instead of fleeing, and she knew how fortunate she had been. She turned and saw a light come on in the house next door. The last thing she wanted was to have the prying eyes of the Misses Marlow at this time of night, so Pippa hurried back indoors. She made sure to bolt all the windows and doors, and then crept back into bed. Jasper stood guard at the door, but even so she did not get any good sleep that night.

But why was that man in the cottage, and what was he looking for?

5

As soon as Pippa had slipped into bed she tried calling Clive again, but there was no answer. She could picture him sitting glued to his laptop, completely oblivious that she was trying to call him. He had never quite been able to think about people when they weren't in his immediate surroundings. It was as though the only world that mattered was the one that was tangible to him. In a way she had been the same. As soon as she had begun her life in London the rest of the world had faded away, including her past. Her childhood had been shed as though it meant nothing to her, but that wasn't the truth. The memories were still fond ones, the nostalgia still warm, but there was now a sense that something had gone awry in her life, that somewhere along the way she had taken the wrong path.

She wished Gordon had still been alive so that she could have spoken to him. He always did know the right things to say. He might have known what was going on here as well, for her mind was filled with questions.

Had Gordon suffered from intruders as well? Was this man merely taking the opportunity to burgle an empty house, or at least a house he thought was empty? Or was there something more sinister going on, something that her grandfather had been hiding? At first it was easy to dismiss the idea, but then she heard Braw Ben talking about the treasure and how he thought Gordon knew more than he was letting on... no... that must have just been an old folk tale. There was no way there was treasure here. People just had too much time on their hands, that was all.

She tried to sleep, but at the slightest hint of a sound she would jerk awake and look around the dim room with wide eyes, her breath caught in her throat. Jasper slept soundly, and she was actually glad that he was in the room with her since she could use him as an alarm. If he growled then she would be worried, but otherwise she could be assured that the house was empty again.

~

Morning arrived and Pippa stretched out her arms. As she drew the curtains and allowed sunlight to pour into the room it was almost easy to believe that nothing had happened the previous night and it had all been a bad dream, but then she went downstairs and peered into the spare room. There was shattered pieces of porcelain over the floor. Her heart caught in her throat again as she remembered the image of the person who had been standing there, who might have attacked her in other circumstances. What had he been looking for? Everything in this room was junk, or at least she thought it was. What was her grandfather hiding?

Without having any friends in Burlybottom on Sea, there was nobody she could turn to for advice or support, but she didn't want to spend the entire day in the cottage, nor did she want to keep this to herself. She thought about the people she had met so far, and decided to pay a visit to John Clarkson's farm. He was a strong man and had evidently known Gordon well, so perhaps he would be able to give her some advice. She grabbed the leash and fastened it on Jasper. This time he did not wriggle so much. She left the house, but as soon as she was turning out of the garden path Martha Marlow opened her door and called out to her. Pippa looked back and was certain that Mindy wasn't far behind.

"Is everything alright Penny? We heard a little bit of commotion last night?" she asked.

Pippa pressed her lips tightly together and frowned. "It's Pippa," she corrected, "and yes, everything is fine. Jasper just wanted some fresh air I think, and I'm not used to all of Grandad's things yet. I just knocked something over, that's all."

"Oh, I see, well if you ever need to come and pay us a visit don't hesitate, we're usually up in the late hours. Neither of us have ever been able to sleep well," she said. Pippa thanked her for the offer and then moved on, not wishing to say anything else because she knew once she told one of these sisters she might as well have told the entire town. The best thing was to just leave well enough alone. Before she left though she did ask them how to get to the farm, explaining that she wanted to see John to ask him something about Jasper. They told her the route and she followed it, walking along the coast and then away from it, following a narrow dirt road that led up to the fields and a forest. It was a picturesque view that offered the very best of England, and again it was like nothing she could find in London. There were parks in London and little spots of greenery, but it was mostly a swamp of grey buildings and glassy skyscrapers, and she thought it a shame that more of the natural beauty couldn't have been preserved.

By the time she reached John's farm she had worked up a bit of a sweat. It seems as though her sessions in the gym on the comfortable treadmill hadn't prepared her for a rigorous walk across uneven terrain. The farm was an old brick building, looking like something out of a fairytale. A large stable rose in the background, as did another outbuilding. There were sounds of cattle lowing and chickens squawking. Jasper put his nose into the air and opened his mouth, as though he was smiling. Perhaps he saw this place as a second home. It was going to have to be his home when she left, because he couldn't very well stay in the cottage alone. A pang of guilt stabbed at her heart. She wondered if Jasper understood what was happening. One moment his owner was with him, the next he was gone. It didn't seem to make much sense.

She rapped her knuckles against the door, but there was no answer. She then moved around the building and followed a path to the stables, hoping to find John nearby. Eventually she heard a grunting sound and found herself standing in the wide doorway of a barn, looking at a floor covered with hay and a cow standing there. John was sitting on a stool, milking it. Pippa winced, a sense of revulsion clinging in her throat. She looked away, as though she was seeing something inappropriate. Jasper barked happily and John turned around, holding a rosy pink teat in each hand. White milk dripped from them and Pippa thought she was going to vomit.

"Pippa! What a pleasure to see you. What can I do for you today? And hello Jasper, I hope you've been taking care of our guest," John said cheerfully.

Pippa tried to avert her gaze, but she found it difficult to tear her eyes away from the sight of him milking a cow. It made it difficult to think. "Would you mind stopping that for a moment?" she asked.

John looked at the udder and sighed. "Okay Rosie, that's enough for the time being."

"Don't they have machines to do that now?" she asked as John dried his hands on a cloth and then stood beside her.

"Yes, but sometimes it's still better to do it by hand. It makes the cows more relaxed, and I like to think that improves the quality of the milk."

Pippa frowned, not convinced by that, but she didn't argue with him about it. He asked her to join him inside. She followed him into the farmhouse, where he appeared to live alone. He offered her some cheese and apple juice, which she declined.

"So what can I do for you? Listen, I am sorry about leaving Jasper with you the other night. He's just been really antsy since Gordon passed on and I thought it would do him good to spend some time in his home."

"It's okay," Pippa said, "actually I wanted to talk to you about something else. Something happened last night… did Grandad ever have any trouble with people breaking into his house?"

John's demeanor changed instantly. He tilted his head forward and pushed his shoulders back. "Was someone in the house?" he asked, his voice lowering.

Pippa nodded. "It was late at night. I don't know who it was. I caught them in the spare room. As soon as Jasper and I appeared he bolted out of the window and ran away. Jasper might have caught his scent but I…" she trailed away, not wanting to admit that she had been afraid to chase the intruder.

"You did the right thing. There's no telling what might have happened if you had gone after him alone. But to answer your question, no, as far as I know Gordon didn't have any trouble. This place isn't used to things like that happening you know. It's a quiet town, and everyone here knows each other for the most part."

"Well they don't know me," Pippa sighed. "I don't know if they were looking for something specific or if they thought the house was empty and were simply trying their luck in case something valuable might have been left behind."

John stroked his chin. "Do you know how they got in?"

"I think one of the windows was loose. I checked everything afterwards and made sure it was locked tightly."

"Well hopefully now that they know you're there they won't come back again, but we should be careful just in case. Nobody in Burlybottom on Sea should ever feel afraid."

Pippa was about to ask him if this could have had anything to do with some treasure, but she caught herself before the words left her lips as she did not want to fall prey to that kind of superstition.

"So this trail Jasper picked up, do you think that it's still there?" John asked.

"I have no idea."

"Might be that we could follow it and find out where this fellow headed. Then we could make sure that he's not going to trouble you again," John said. He was already grabbing his coat, so Pippa felt as though she had no choice but to agree.

∼

They walked back to the cottage with Jasper ambling along in front of them. They were speaking idly about the farm, and John was telling her what a lot of work it was. Pippa found her admiration growing for him. To put in as many hours as he did toiling away with the animals and the land was impressive and certainly not something that she could ever picture herself doing.

"I like knowing that there comes an hour in the day when I can finish working," she said.

"Well that's the thing I suppose; I don't see it as work. My family has been taking care of the land for generations. It's practically my birthright, and I couldn't imagine doing anything else," he said.

They reached the cottage and Pippa glanced up, noticing how the Marlow sisters were peeking out of their curtains. She huffed and shook her head. John looked up and noticed what was happening, but he just chuckled.

"I assume you have become acquainted with your neighbors?" he asked.

"Do they do anything other than stare out of their windows? You'd think they would get a hobby or something."

"I think people are their hobby. They just like taking an interest in the world around them. They're harmless really."

Pippa twisted her lips in scorn, for she wasn't sure about that. Sometimes spreading rumor and gossip could be more harmful than anyone realized. She didn't get a chance to say this to John though, because Jasper was fussing around the garden and then his head shot up and his ears pricked up too.

"Looks like he's sensed something," John said. They walked on. Pippa didn't feel as scared as she had the previous night, although she was not sure if it was because daylight surrounded them, or if it was because John was there. She glanced toward him, admiring the broad shoulders and the muscles that had been knotted together from hard work. His palms were hard and calloused, his fingers thick, not the slender, nimble things that danced across a keyboard like Clive's. John was the kind of man that you simply didn't find in the world any longer, a throwback to a simpler time, and she was grateful for this as she couldn't imagine Clive coming on this journey with her. He couldn't even handle the spiders that crept into his flat, often squealing and hiding while she took care of them.

"So what do you think you're going to do with Gordon's cottage then?" John asked as they walked along the coast, away from the beach to the part of the sea where the fishing boats trawled the water.

"I'll probably sell it. I'm just trying to go through everything at the moment. He had a lot of stuff."

John chuckled. "Yes, Gordon did like collecting things," he said. There it was again, this sense of intimacy that the people here had with her grandad, the thing that she lacked.

"If there's anything you want then you can come by and take it. I'm sure he would have wanted you to have something of his, aside from Jasper," Pippa said.

"Oh I couldn't do that. He left it all to you. You are his family after all," John said earnestly. Pippa just scoffed.

"And what does that even mean? Everyone here knew him better than I did."

"Family is family," John said, as though that explained everything and she shouldn't be concerned with it at all. It still gnawed in the back of Pippa's mind though, and she wondered if she would ever be able to shake this feeling of guilt.

She was able to forget about it for the time being though as Jasper led them along a winding path that led them over some jagged rocks. The going was not easy, and Pippa had to stretch out her hand and press against the rocky outcrop for support. Jasper was agile and didn't seem to suffer any difficulty at all. The path then became a little easier as there was a small jetty and wooden boards, and it led to a hut.

"This used to be used by fishermen when the trade was bigger here," John said, lowering his voice. The shack was weathered and was in such a state that it looked as though a strong wind would have been able to blow it down. There were trees behind it and a small opening in the rocks where the sapphire sea was visible. John crept toward the shack and held up his hand, indicating for Pippa to remain still. Jasper moved with John, the two of them looking as though they shared a telepathic bond. Pippa swallowed a lump in her throat as she thought about what might be waiting for her in the shack. John reached the door. Nobody had appeared yet, but had they heard John approach? Were they waiting to attack now? Might they have a gun?

Pippa gasped and felt herself go rigid with fright as John reached out and opened the door. It swung open and Pippa ducked, almost expecting a madman to come running out flailing a weapon of some sort, but there wasn't anything like that. John beckoned her forward with a waving hand. When she approached she saw a pile of dark clothes and bits of food left strewn about. There was definitely signs of life, signs that someone had made this their home, but they weren't here at the moment.

"Are these what your intruder was wearing?" John asked, gesturing to the clothes. Jasper had his nose buried into them.

"I don't know. It was dark. I couldn't make out much detail, but Jasper certainly seems to think so," she said.

"Well, perhaps being discovered put enough of a fright into him that he left. He's certainly not here at the moment after all," John said. With nothing else to investigate they left and returned to the cottage, although as they were walking back Pippa felt an itch on the back of her neck, as though someone was watching them. Neither Jasper nor John acted as though anything was amiss though, so she did not let it faze her.

When they reached the cottage John turned to her. "If you like you can stay at the farmhouse with me. I have the room, just so that you feel safe."

Pippa blushed. She wondered what Clive would have thought about that. "No, I'm sure it's fine. Like you said, it was probably just someone who saw an opportunity but has been scared away now. As long as I have Jasper I'm sure I'll be fine."

"Okay, but don't hesitate to call me in case there's any trouble again, right?" he said. Pippa nodded.

"I promise."

John then smiled and walked away. He cast a quick wave to the Marlow sisters next door, and Pippa cringed, knowing the kinds of theories they would spin about why Pippa and John had been spending time together. That was the last thing on her mind though. At least she had found where this intruder was staying, and by the look of it there was only one of him. It was probably just some vagrant who was trying his luck, although she did wonder if she should try and get back to London as soon as possible. She didn't enjoy fear ruling her life, but she couldn't quite bring herself to leave yet.

The phone in the cottage rang. It was a loud, shrill ring that filled the cavernous rooms and almost made the entire house shake. Pippa almost jumped out of skin. She handled the receiver, finding it quaint compared to the sleek cell phones that most people used nowadays.

"Hello, is this Ms. Finn?"

"Yes, speaking, who is calling?" Pippa asked. She was always wary of anyone calling her that she did not recognize, and she wondered how anyone had managed with telephones before. At least with a cell phone she could look up any number she did not recognize.

"I'm just with the estate agents. I was wondering if there was any progress with the sale of the cottage." The voice was that of a man. It was rough and coarse, and Pippa couldn't shake the feeling that something was amiss.

Surely the estate agents would have called her on her mobile phone, and this person would have introduced himself by name.

"I'm sorry, who exactly is calling? I have been talking to someone called Donna previously," Pippa said, plucking a fictitious name out of the air.

"I'm afraid Donna had some other business to attend to, so I'm handling the call," he said. Pippa felt a mixture of smugness and anxiety. She had caught him in a trap, but that meant that he might be dangerous. Her tone turned icy.

"Were you in the cottage last night?" she asked.

"I don't know what you're talking about."

"There is no Donna. I made that name up. You're not with the estate agents at all. Who are you and what do you want?" Pippa shook with a cocktail of anger and fear. Her voice was sharp on the phone, as though she was sending daggers toward him. The man's tone changed as well. There was a cruel sneer to his voice.

"You need to leave the house and put it on the market. The sooner the better," they said, and then hung up before Pippa could ask them any further questions. Well, this was definitely not someone who was just taking the opportunity to burgle an empty house.

6

Pippa staggered to the pub because she needed a drink and she didn't care where it came from. Braw Ben chuckled as she walked in and asked her if she was looking for some more strange food. A couple of men at the bar laughed, but Pippa just walked to the end of the bar and asked for some wine. Her face was pale and her eyes were lined with terror. Braw Ben tried to make some small talk, but she wasn't responding. He frowned and looked at her more closely.

"Are you alright? You look like you've seen a ghost," he said. Pippa's throat was dry and even after she drank some wine that scratchy feeling did not go away. The events had shaken her so much, and she found that she needed to talk about it with someone, anyone, even Braw Ben.

"I... there was someone in the house last night. I don't know what they tried to steal, but they were looking for something. And then I just received a phone call from someone. They wouldn't tell me who they were, but they said that I should leave." Her trembling hand reached out to clutch the wine glass and she brought it to her lips, hoping that the dazed effect would take hold soon.

"Oh you can't leave," Braw Ben said, looking stern as he shook his head. "Whoever they are, they sound like a bully. No, you can't let them get the better of you. There's something in that house alright. You have to find out what it is. It has to be something to do with the treasure. I knew Gordon knew something! If only he would have told me..." Braw Ben slapped his palm against the counter and then frowned. He then looked at Pippa directly. "He left something there for you Pippa, don't you see? That's why you're here. He wanted you to find something, something that he knew other people wanted."

"I don't know..." Pippa said weakly as she drank more wine. She had a couple of glasses with these thoughts dancing through her mind, and then she walked back to the cottage. The sun was dipping below the horizon. The sky was streaked with red. She glanced around, afraid that someone was following her. Jasper didn't react to anything though. She went inside and checked the doors and windows again, not satisfied until she had tested that all of them were secure.

Was it truly possible that her grandfather had sent her to this place for a reason, that there was something he could only trust with her? It didn't seem possible, especially when there were so many people in Burlybottom on Sea that he was closer to. She went into the spare room and cleaned up the shattered pieces of the broken ornament and then sat at his desk. There was an album in one of the drawers that had photos and newspaper clippings about his time in the war, about the deeds he had performed. As she read about how he had put his own life on the line to save other people, how he had run into danger fearlessly to defend his country she wondered how they could have been related. There was a bond of blood, but she had never felt more distance between them. She wasn't anything like him. She was ambitious and focused, and she didn't think she was the type of person to ever go to war. Gordon had been a hero, but there were no newspaper articles written about her. There wasn't anyone who was going to look back at pictures of her and feel a swell of pride. It was almost as though she wasn't related to him at all, as though he should have had a different granddaughter, one who he could actually have been proud of.

As she flicked through the album she found a letter written by him in a crude hand. The paper was smudged with dirt. He had written it in another country while he served in the army. Her eyes danced across the words, trying to imagine him hunkered down in a trench somewhere, cold and starving, scared and alone under the stars.

I'm trying not to be scared. They train us not to be scared, but how can you train the fear out of a man? I think it's impossible. Jimmy keeps talking about running away. I catch him glancing at the forest sometimes and I know he's only one moment away from fleeing into the darkness. Sometimes I think about joining him, but I couldn't bear the shame. I'm here for a reason and I just have to keep going. I'm here doing God's work. I have to remember that. He's looking out for me, just as all of you are. I know that you're looking up at the same stars as I am, and that's what keeps me going. Someday soon I shall be with you again and we will have a jolly time together. I feel lucky because there are some men here who don't have a family waiting for them at home. I can see the hopelessness in their eyes. I'm fighting for you, and I will return. I promise. I have to remember that you can't be brave unless you're scared first. I will see you soon,

Gordy

Pippa wiped a tear away, unsure when it had begun to spill down her cheek. She felt bad. Family had meant so much to him, yet in his final days he had been forgotten and left behind, having to form connections with his neighbors and friends because his family had forsaken him. After everything he had done, everything he had accomplished he had ended up alone, and it was all her fault. If she had just been a little more attentive, a little more considerate then she might have been able to come and visit him. Telling herself that she was busy was just an excuse. She had had time for the gym and to grab cocktails with friends. There was always time, but never a willingness to spend it with the people who mattered.

And now it was too late.

But was there something here that her grandfather had left for her, something that he could only trust with a family member? If there was then she couldn't allow it to fall into the hands of someone who did not deserve it. She could not forsake Gordon again. She gathered her inner strength and breathed deeply, telling herself that fear was not a reason to let this get the better of her. Even though she didn't see any resemblance to her grandfather she knew that she was his relation. That meant all the qualities he had possessed were within her, and she just had to look inside herself to find them. She could be brave too if she wanted. He had gone over to another country when he was barely old enough to grow a beard to fight an inhumane war, the least she could do was go in search of someone who broke into his house. Whoever called her on the phone wanted her gone, but she wasn't going to listen to them. She needed answers and there was only one place to find them; the shack. She needed to find whoever stayed there and get them to tell her the truth, and only then would she know what she could do with the cottage.

She was tempted to call John, but the hour was late and besides, she was a modern, independent woman. But she did need something else. She looked around and found something that had caught her eye earlier. It was a gun, a pistol with a long barrel. She picked it up. It was heavier than she expected. She had never carried a gun before. In fact she had always been disgusted by the existence of them and thought that war was an ugly thing, but she wasn't prepared to go and confront this man unarmed. If nothing else it would put the fear of God into him, and might buy her a few moments if he decided to attack her.

Pippa's heart beat fiercely as she took Jasper outside again and traced a path back to the shack. The sun had dipped fully below the horizon now and the night had taken on a different air. Fear whispered around her and she wondered if this was how her grandfather had felt when he had been stalking through territory in a foreign land, knowing that the enemy was nearby and one wrong noise would bring thunder crashing down around him.

The wind whipped around the coastline and it made the way even more treacherous. The tide had crept up the beach. The stars were a chaotic pattern in the night sky, and the moon was just a silver crescent. London would have been twinkling as brightly as the night sky, but Burlybottom on Sea was dark, as though it was entirely asleep. The sea was as dark as wine, and it became difficult to see where she was walking, but Pippa wasn't about to relent now. This village was not going to get the better of her. The same blood that flowed through her grandfather was the blood that flowed through her, and she could do this. She *could* do this.

Pippa reached the shack. Jasper wasn't growling yet, so she thought she might be safe. If the man wasn't here then she didn't know what she was going to do about it. Going to the police was the obvious option, but she was certain they had better things to do than investigate a break in to a home where nothing was taken. The most they would do was take a report and let it languish in some drawer somewhere. When she looked into the shack the pile of clothes was gone. Jasper sniffed around, and then he stiffened. Pippa knew that something was wrong. She crept out of the shack and then saw him, illuminated by the pale light of the moon. He stood on a ridge that overlooked the sea. The water sloshed against the coast and she became rigid with fear. She clutched the gun tightly and approached the man, telling herself that he was just a man, not a monster.

As she grew closer she saw him more clearly. He was not wearing a balaclava now. His face was narrow and he had a pencil thin mustache. His hair was black and trim, and his eyes were as black as coal. Pippa followed her fear and walked up to him so that she could speak to him. She tried to keep her gaze leveled at his eyes, but it was difficult to do when he had this sneering façade. He spoke and she listened carefully, trying to gauge whether this was the same man who had spoken to her on the telephone, or if there was someone else involved.

"So, you have found me," he said. Did he have a slight accent, or was Pippa imagining it.

"Yes, I did. Who are you and what do you want? Why were you in my grandfather's house?" she asked, the questions punching through the air like bullets being fired from a machine gun. The man stared at her, completely unfazed.

"I am an… interested party. I was in your grandfather's house looking for something, something that did not belong to him."

"What is it? Tell me what you wanted."

The man just smiled, the corners of his lips tilting upwards in a vague hint of amusement. "I think perhaps you already know. He left you the house, yes? Surely he would have told you."

"He didn't tell me anything. I… we… didn't speak much."

"Please, you were his granddaughter. I know you are lying to me."

"I'm not, and I don't have to justify myself to you. Tell me what's going on here or I'll… I'll shoot," she said, her voice faltering and wavering as she raised the gun, producing it from where it had been hidden behind her back. Her hand trembled and the gun suddenly felt as heavy as an anchor, as though it was dragging her arm down to the ground. Jasper was growling beside her, his teeth bared, although he hadn't yet made any attempt to attack this man. The man looked at the gun and arched an eyebrow. Pippa had hoped that he would show a little more fear than this.

"I don't think you know why you're here. Your grandfather wasn't the man you think he was."

"He was a hero," Pippa said, suddenly filled with pride and a need to defend a man who could not defend himself.

The man's face twisted in disgust and he spat. Fury poured out of his eyes. "You do not know the meaning of the word. He's a thief, just like the rest of them. If you have any sense of justice then you will take me back to that cottage right now and help me find what I am looking for."

"We're not going anywhere," Pippa said. She wanted herself to sound proud and intimidating, but instead her voice came out as reedy.

"You should. You should go back to your life before this. Your grandfather involved you in something that you don't know anything about. We're going to go back to the cottage and you're going to let me look through anything I want," he said. His voice had a dangerous edge to it and she became worried about what he might be capable of. Before she could do anything he moved, as quick as a flash, and he was striding toward her. Pippa froze in shock and terror and then she felt his hand on her arm, his fingers digging into her flesh. A scream bellowed from the depths of her throat and Jasper leapt up and sunk his teeth into the man's arm, growling loudly. Then there was a shot of thunder through the air as well, a crack that sent a tremor through the world as her finger pulled the trigger. It was just a twitch, a reflex, she hadn't even been aware that it happened, but the man staggered back nonetheless, crying out in pain. His clothes were so dark she couldn't see the spread of blood that must have been oozing out of him. The barrel of the gun trembled. He had been so close to her that there wasn't any way she could have missed, but she felt sick and shocked by the fact that she had just shot a man. She wanted to rush up to him, to check if he was okay, but he was already losing his balance and stepping back. The wind whipped around him and the ground was flecked with spray from the rising tide. Pippa watched helplessly as he slipped back and fell. His scream was horrifying and she rushed to the edge, looking down into the dark depths of the water, but there was no trace of him, only the echo of his scream that soon faded. Pippa moved so quickly that she stumbled and fell as well, losing her footing on the slippery ground. Her mind was hazy from what had just happened and she almost became delirious. The gun fell from her hand, landing with a dull thud, while her head cracked against a sharp rock. Pain blazed through her and then she was staring up at the stars, thinking about so many things, while her thoughts became heavy and the darkness encroached upon her. The last thing she saw was Jasper sniffing around her and licking her, but then everything went dark.

7

Pippa's mind was chaotic in her forced slumber. She could think of nothing but that terrible moment where the reverberation of the gun had shot up her arm and the man had gone staggering back, claimed by the water. The violent current had shown no mercy, and had claimed the man and the secrets he held. Pippa had so many questions and not enough answers, and now she wasn't sure if she was ever going to get any of them. It seemed as though her grandfather was not the only one to take secrets to his grave.

There was a pinprick of light that she followed. She opened her eyes. Her mind swam and her movements were sluggish. The lights were bright and she gasped for breath as she pushed herself into a sitting position, and she was quite surprised to find herself not surrounded by the open air and the stars, but by the watchful eyes of the people of Burlybottom on Sea. She cowered a little out of shock, but then smiled when she saw John's face.

"What... what am I doing here?" she asked.

"Jasper came to find me. He trailed his leash along and I knew something must have happened if he was alone. You were lucky he was with you," John said. "I followed the trail back to the shack and saw you lying there. What were you thinking going back there alone?"

"I... I just wanted to find out what was going on," Pippa said, rubbing her temples and the bridge of her nose. There was a pulsing ache that would not relent and she wondered if she had a concussion.

"I brought you back here. Callie bandaged your head, and Braw stoked the fire for you to keep you warm. You're safe now," John said, although there was a terse edge to his voice that belied his charming manner from before. Pippa glanced around and offered them a grateful smile. Callie looked worried, while Braw Ben was more relaxed.

"Thank you," Pippa said, although she wasn't sure what she had done to deserve such treatment.

"So did you find him?" John asked, folding his arm across his chest.

Whatever color had returned to Pippa's cheeks now drained again as she took a deep breath. A look of horror, pain, and shame came over her eyes as she thought about what happened to the man.

"I… I killed him. I shot him," she said, and then looked around herself for the gun.

"With this?" Braw Ben asked, picking up the gun that had rested on the counter. He twisted it around and looked at the barrel. Pippa gasped with fright at how casual he was acting with it. She remembered the sound of the shot and the feeling of the power running up her arm. It was the kind of thing that couldn't be allowed in the hands of an untrained person.

"Y-yes," Pippa said, trying to wrest her gaze away from the gun. To her surprise Braw Ben laughed.

"You couldn't have killed him with this Pippa. It's only a ceremonial piece. Any bullet inside would have been a blank. You might have hurt him, but if he died it's the sea that killed him, and the sea metes out its own justice. Whoever he was, it sounds like he deserved it," Braw Ben said. Pippa felt a little better when she heard this, although she still didn't like how close she had come to death herself. It could easily have been her that was flung over that ridge and tossed into the abyss of the sea. Pippa nodded and drank some water that Callie handed to her. She touched the bandage that wrapped around the crown of her head and winced.

"You got quite a lump. It might take a few days to go down," Callie said.

"It looks like we've got some excitement in Burlybottom on Sea though. I wonder what that man wanted," Braw

Ben said.

"I have no idea," Pippa said reluctantly. She then looked at the people around her and furrowed her brow. "Why did you all help me? I haven't exactly been the friendliest person to you all."

The others all looked at each other, as though none of them wanted to actually admit that she had been brash and unkind. It took Braw Ben to break the silence, as he was not a man who was afraid of speaking his mind. "The thing is Pippa that we take care of our own, and like it or not, you're one of us," he said with a wide smile. Pippa looked at the others and saw accepting nods, although John's quickly faded and was replaced by his stern look. She found herself smiling too. It had been a long time since she had been accepted into a place just for being herself, and while she wasn't sure she deserved this treatment, she was glad that she had people looking out for her. Life in London could be isolated and lonely. It was nice to remember what it was like to be a part of a community.

She thanked them all and Braw Ben insisted that she have something to eat. He produced a sandwich with greasy strips of bacon that was the unhealthiest thing she had eaten in a long time, but after they had saved her she didn't feel like she could turn it down, and in truth her stomach grumbled and craved for something like this anyway. There were always moments in life when it was acceptable to indulge oneself. After this she said that she needed to get back to the cottage. John said that he would escort her, in case she lost her balance again.

They walked in brisk silence. John could be intimidating when he wanted.

"So did you learn anything at all from him?" he asked eventually as they approached the cottage.

"Not really… just that he was looking for something, something specific. He said Grandad had taken it a long time ago, but he wouldn't tell me what. He seemed to think that I knew what he was looking for. I don't suppose Grandad told you anything that might make sense here?" she asked, looking up at him with hope.

John shook his head. "Nothing that comes to mind anyway. Whatever he was hiding it's in that cottage though, and you're the only one who can find it. He brought you back here for a reason Pippa," he said.

Pippa gulped. Was it actually possible that this had something to do with the treasure? She would have to look into the stories more and determine if there was any truth to what Braw Ben said. John walked her right to the front door.

"Listen Pippa, if you ever do anything like this again please tell me first. You shouldn't have gone there alone. Anything might have happened. That man was dangerous. I wouldn't like anything to happen to you," he said.

Pippa looked up at him and for a moment she lost herself in the glint of his blue eyes. Her heart fluttered and she felt a hazy feeling in her mind. It wasn't anything like she had felt before and she started to think that she was suffering from the effects of her head wound.

"I don't think anything like this is ever going to happen again," Pippa said.

"Good," John replied, and then he bid her goodnight. Pippa watched him walk away and wondered if this sense of protection he had over her was due to an obligation he had made to her grandfather, a duty because the people of the community looked out for each other, or perhaps something more. There was a hint of her smile at the last thought, but then she pushed it away, telling herself that she shouldn't think like this. Clive was waiting for her back in London after all, although London had never seemed so far away. It was strange to think of her life back in London, so filled with routine and rigor, when out here it was dripping with mystery and intrigue.

She walked through the house and sighed, standing in the middle of the hallway, surrounded by all of Gordon's things.

"What were you hiding here Grandad?" she asked. There was no reply of course, but Jasper came up to her and licked her hand. Pippa found herself petting the dog back, ruffling his soft curly fur, and found herself thinking about her time as a girl when she had come to this cottage.

Had there been something that her grandfather had told her back then that might shed some light on all of this? If there was it did not come to mind immediately. She trudged upstairs and fell into bed, this time falling asleep immediately.

8

It was morning. Pippa's head still ached, but she felt better. The night had passed without incident and there was no sign that anyone had tried to break in again. Pippa assumed that the man was working alone, but if there was indeed something valuable hidden in the cottage then it was possible that other people might come looking for it, which meant that Pippa was going to have to try and figure out what was so valuable quickly. The problem was it could have been anything, and Pippa wasn't really sure where to begin. But first she had to call Clive.

This time he did answer. It was always easier to get a hold of him in the morning.

"Hey Pippa, what's going on? Are you ready to return home yet?"

She hesitated telling him the truth. Clive never handled this kind of thing well and he probably would have gotten a little overprotective, and he would have definitely wanted her to head back to London.

"Not yet. Things are taking a little longer here than I first thought. Grandad has a lot of stuff and I really want to make sure that none of it is a hidden gem."

"That makes sense I guess. Do you really think he would have had anything valuable? You know what old people are like, they hoard any old junk. I don't think any of them have ever heard of being a minimalist," he said with a biting laugh.

"Something tells me there just might be. I'll keep you updated. I can't really give you a timeframe about how long I'll be though."

"No worries. I have plenty of things to keep me busy anyway," he said. Perhaps it was unfair of her, but she almost wanted him to get angry, just once, just to show that he really cared. There were times when it felt as though he was never really bothered if she was around or not. It might have been because he appreciated her freedom and allowed Pippa her liberty, but there were times when she would have liked to feel his anguish at being separated from her. He had never looked as concerned as John had, for example. But perhaps she was being silly anyway. She had had an intense few days and now was not the time to be introspective.

"I'm sure you do."

"Better you than me as well. I can't imagine what it's like to be around all those people."

"They're not all bad," Pippa said, thinking about the kindness she had been shown ever since she had arrived. None of them had been rude to her, and all of them had been friendly. There was no need for Clive to speak about them like that, but it wasn't worth chastising him for it.

"If you say so. Listen, I need to go because I have a conference call. I'll speak to you later," he said, and then had hung up even before she had a chance to say goodbye. She placed the cell phone down on the table and sighed, looking at the sleek, black device. Right now it was the only thing linking her to her life back in London. At some point she was going to have to go back there and tell Clive all that had happened but how, would he believe her? Even she found it difficult to believe that she had tracked down an intruder in the dark of night. It was so out of character for her, but then again sometimes in times of distress people find hidden aspects of themselves. It must have been the same with Gordon as well. He wouldn't have grown up being a soldier, but would have developed the skills he needed to survive over there… but had he brought something back from the war with him?

She was about to search the ornaments again, beginning the arduous task of sifting through her grandfather's life in the hope of finding... what, exactly? Some treasure? She wasn't even sure if that was what the man had been looking for. It was logical to assume that it might have been something from her grandfather's years of serving in the army, but that was only an assumption. He had lived a long life, longer than most, and a lot of it was a mystery to her. She had been so focused on her own life and her own ambition that she hadn't paid proper care to learn about him. Did she even know what his favorite color was? It was these simple little things that always got lost on the way though. She thought perhaps she would just have to get to know the people of Burlybottom on Sea a little better as well in the hope that they might tell her something she needed to know about her grandfather.

Before she could go into the spare room and begin searching through all the artifacts of her grandfather's life, Jasper began scratching at the door, wanting a walk again.

"Alright Jasper, stop your fussing," she said, and fetched the leash. She took a different path this time, wanting to avoid the shack. She shuddered at the memory. She walked along the coast. The water had always seemed like a thing of beauty to her, a glittering wonder that was endless in its depths and its mysteries, but now she had learned that it was also cruel and violent, that it could bring a man to his end without a second thought.

Who am I?

The thought ran through her mind, crackling like a bolt of electricity. She may not have been responsible for the man's death, but she had still gone there with a gun. She had still been willing to do the unthinkable. Had this potential always been inside her, or was it something that this place had drawn out? Was it the same thing her grandfather had experienced during the war? He must have been faced with so many difficult situations then and he must have wondered who he was. He had his family to anchor him, to remind him what he was fighting for and what he was eventually going to return home to. What did she have?

There was Clive, but their relationship was no great passionate love affair. It was comfortable and beneficial. She had her job and her investments, but what did those mean in the grand scheme of things? It wasn't as though she was going to be remembered for doing anything heroic, or had anything to pull herself back from the brink. Rationally she knew that she should just leave this place behind and sell the house and continue with her life in London, but there was something about this place that called to her. She had not been the best granddaughter she could have been, but she could make up for that now. Her Grandad had tasked her to protect something… she didn't know what… but she would protect it for him. She would make him proud, as proud as he should have been during his life.

Eventually Jasper tugged at the leash and forced her to continue on the walk, taking her away from the beach and the sea, and she hoped that in time she would be able to forget the image of that man slipping off the ridge just as easily as she could turn away from the coastline.

∼

Pippa hadn't been intending to head to the church, but she ended up there anyway. It was a small building, not like the large structures in London that were always shown on TV. This was a humble building set to fulfil the spiritual needs of the community. The grounds were filled with colorful flowers, and to the rear was a cemetery with tombstones poking up, each of them the final statement of a life that was well lived. Pippa took Jasper through this cemetery and glanced at the names, none of which she recognized. A lot of them were overgrown with moss or had weathered with age, and the names were barely legible. The church door opened and the vicar emerged, greeting Pippa with a wave.

"Good day Pippa, how are you feeling?"

"I'm well, thank you Reverend," she replied. The bandage was gone from her head and the lump was in the process of receding. She had put plenty of ice on it, although there was still a dull ache of pain.

"I heard what happened," George said. Pippa wondered if this was the Marlow sisters' doing again, or if it had come from another source. She supposed there was no end to the possibilities. John didn't seem the type to let the information slip out in casual conversation, but Callie was cheerful enough that she might not have understood the importance of it, and Braw Ben seemed eager to tell anyone about the treasure. "I'm glad the Lord was watching over you."

Pippa gave him a polite smile. "I have to confess something to you Reverend, I've never been very religious. In fact I'm not sure if it's appropriate for me to be here."

George gave her a reassuring smile and clasped his hands together. "The church is open to everyone, as is God's love. I don't know what could have possessed someone to want to break into Gordon's house, but I am sorry it happened. Burlybottom on Sea is usually such a quiet, peaceful place. It's something we pride ourselves on."

"Well, hopefully it won't happen again."

"Would you like to see your grandfather?" he asked. Pippa was taken aback and almost wondered how it was possible, before she realized that George was speaking about the grave. Pippa closed her open mouth and then nodded. George took her through the cemetery to a plot of land at the rear area. It was shrouded by trees, and poppies grew around the tombstone. There was a fresh one and a weathered one. The fresh one was her grandfather's, and as she stood before the grave she was filled with emotion. It was overwhelming. She hadn't expected it to hit her like a flood.

"I think they're at peace now together. Do you happen to remember your grandmother?" he asked.

"Not really. She died when I was very young. Grandad was alone for such a long time."

"Yes, he was a pious and loyal man. You know, once he confessed to me that he had never had much love for the Church. I suppose many men who have seen the horrors of war feel the same way. But he said that his wife's devotion had rubbed off on him and he came for her. It's remarkable how so much love can last in a man, isn't it?"

"Yes, it is…" she said, and choked on her emotion. Jasper lay down and placed his paws on top of each other at the grave of his master.

"Reverend, did Grandad speak about his time in the war with you?" she asked.

George shook his head. "Not directly. In truth I think it was something that he liked to forget. He did a proud duty, but war is an ugly thing. He preferred to try and help people. That was how he liked to make the world a better place. I did make it clear to him that if there was anything he ever wanted to share with me then I was always open to talking about it, but he just looked at me with this really grim look in his eyes and he shook his head. He told me that I wouldn't want to know what he had done in the war. It's a shame. I think he carried many burdens. He was a strong man, your grandad, but at least he is at peace now. There is no war where he has gone."

Pippa nodded. "I just wondered if he had mentioned anything special. The man I found said that he was looking for something. I wondered if Grandad had found anything that he brought back with him from the war."

"If there was anything like that then he didn't mention it to me. I shouldn't put too much stock into what men like those say though. Chances are they don't know what they're talking about and are just trying to scare you. Gordon was a good man. He wouldn't have taken anything that wasn't his."

"I guess so," Pippa said.

A few moments of silence passed between them. "I know that you're not very religious yourself, but I want to extend to you the same invitation I extended to Gordon. You're always welcome here, whether just to sit and take some time to reflect on life, or to talk about anything that is troubling you."

Pippa thought back to the moment her finger had squeezed the trigger. Did that make her a bad person? Did the fact that Gordon had served in a war make him a bad person too? She kept her mouth closed for the time being though, not wishing to speak to George about this.

"I'll think about it," she said. "What was his memorial service like?"

"Oh it was wonderful, well, as wonderful as such a thing can be. The whole village turned out for him and everyone had such nice things to say about him. We sang his favorite hymns. I think he would have been happy with how it turned out. It's a shame that you couldn't have been here," George said.

Pippa closed her eyes and wished that things could have been different. Now that she was standing in front of his grave she couldn't believe that anything had ever been more important than her grandfather. She remembered how he used to skim stones with her and pretend that the ocean was going to catch them and drag them deep into the ocean. She remembered how he used to buy her fish and chips and take her by the hand as they walked through the village, and how the summers spent in Burlybottom on Sea had been the best times of her life.

Somewhere along the way she had gotten too old for them and had pushed them away. George left her to stand alone and she bowed her head. Tears crawled down her cheeks.

"I'm sorry Grandad," she sobbed, but she would find a way to make it up to him.

∼

THANK YOU FOR CHOOSING A PUREREAD BOOK!

We hope you enjoyed the story, and as a way to thank you for choosing PureRead we'd like to send you this free Special Edition Cozy, and other fun reader rewards…

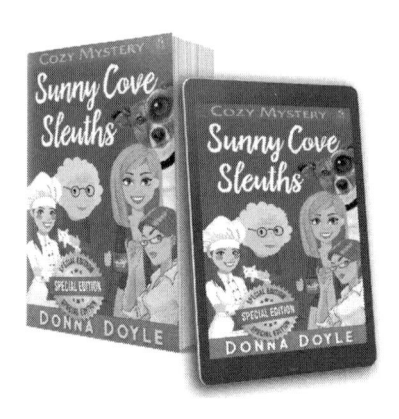

Click Here to download your free Cozy Mystery
PureRead.com/cozy

Thanks again for reading.

See you soon!

OUR GIFT TO YOU

AS A WAY TO SAY THANK YOU WE WOULD LOVE TO SEND YOU THIS SPECIAL EDITION COZY MYSTERY FREE OF CHARGE.

Our Reader List is 100% FREE

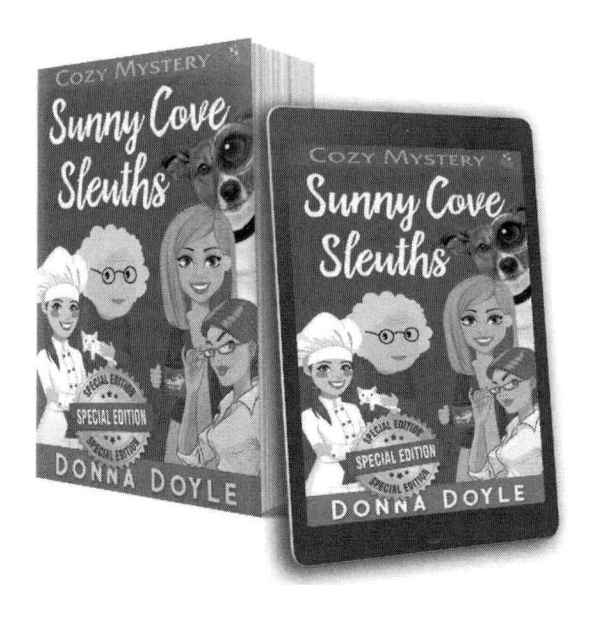

Click Here to download your free Cozy Mystery
PureRead.com/cozy

At PureRead we publish books you can trust. Great tales without smut or swearing, but with all of the mystery and romance you expect from a great story.

Be the first to know when we release new books, take part in our fun competitions, and get surprise free books in your inbox by signing up to our Reader list.

As a thank you you'll receive this exclusive Special Edition Cozy available only to our subscribers...

Click Here to download your free Cozy Mystery
PureRead.com/cozy

Thanks again for reading.
See you soon!